ESCAPE

ESCAPE

Mona Dunckel

illustrated by
Mary Ann Lumm

JOURNEY
B O O K S™
Greenville, South Carolina

Library of Congress Cataloging-in-Publication Data

Dunckel, Mona 1947-
 Escape / Mona Dunckel ; illustrated by Mary Ann Lumm.
  p. cm.
 Summary: When rebel soldiers arrest and plan to execute his
father, a missionary in Ethiopia, Charlie must face sudden dangers
while also trusting those who attempt a rescue.
 ISBN 1-57924-068-2
 [1. Escapes—Fiction. 2. Ethiopia—Fiction. 3. Missionaries—
Fiction. 4. Christian life—Fiction.] I. Lumm, Mary Ann, ill.
II. Title.
PZ7.D9133Es 1998
[Fic]—dc21 98-35287
  CIP
  AC

Escape

Edited by Debbie L. Parker
Designed by Duane A. Nichols

© 1998 Journey Books
Published by Bob Jones University Press
Greenville, South Carolina 29614

Printed in the United States of America

ISBN 1-57924-068-2

15 14 13 12 11 10 9 8 7 6 5 4 3 2 1

For Mom and Dad
who gave me a love for books
and a love for missions

Contents

1   As Usual?

"Charlie, it's time to get up."

Charlie rolled over and stretched. "Okay, Mom," he called.

He lay in bed for several minutes more, just listening. His mother was talking to his baby sister, and Carrie was jabbering happily back.

His father hummed as he walked down the hall. But there was something quieter than usual about his father's hum. And his step seemed quicker.

Charlie had the feeling that something was different about today.

He couldn't hear any sounds coming from the kitchen. But he could tell that Gifati, the girl who helped them, had already been busy. The warm sweet scent of cinnamon filled his room.

Mandazi, thought Charlie as he hopped out of bed. The doughnutlike *mandazi* were his favorite breakfast sweet.

He didn't have to choose his clothes as he had when he lived in the United States. In Ethiopia, getting dressed for school meant putting on the white shirt, tie, and gray shorts of his uniform. He carefully pulled up the gray knee socks with the dark blue stripes. Then he smoothed his hair down with his hands.

As he passed by his shelves, Charlie paused. He ran a hand over the red fire engine his grandfather had sent him for his birthday.

He rolled up the hose—it could squirt real water—and flicked the lights on and off. Then he hurried toward the kitchen.

His parents were just sitting down at the table for breakfast. His father gave Charlie's ear a little tug. "Good morning, Son."

"Morning, Dad." Charlie sat down quickly and folded his hands while his father prayed. As soon as the prayer was finished, Charlie reached for the heaping plate of *mandazi*.

"Charlie, you know that you need to eat the rest of your breakfast first," his mother said.

Charlie did know. But corn flakes, even with slices of thick, stubby finger bananas could not match the sweet cinnamon doughnuts. He poured the milk over his cereal and listened to what his parents were saying.

They were discussing politics again, and the "growing unrest" in Ethiopia. Lately, they often talked about the government. He didn't understand it.

But today his mother said something strange. "I just don't know what will happen to the church if . . . " She glanced at Charlie and stopped.

Father's voice was calm. "God will look out for His own," he said.

Charlie took a long drink of cold milk. He wondered why his mother's voice had sounded quivery.

He was finishing his third piece of *mandazi* when a polite knock came at the gate. Charlie popped up from his chair.

He called to his friend. "Wandaro!" Then he hurried to brush his teeth and pull on his navy blue vest.

"Bye, Mom," he said. On his way through the kitchen, he grabbed two more *mandazi*. He dashed out the door and through the gate.

"Here." Charlie handed Wandaro one of the *mandazi*.

"What a good friend," said Wandaro with a big smile. He was dressed exactly like Charlie.

As they walked, they silently munched their doughnuts.

Then Charlie said, "What shall we do after school?"

Wandaro spoke with his mouth full. He said something that sounded like "Look for treasure."

Charlie and Wandaro were joined by other friends along the way. Each one was dressed in the gray shorts, tie, and navy vest of his school uniform. Ebbe and his brother Biru hurried to catch up with them. Biru was seven, like Charlie, but he had just started school. His parents had been unable to afford the uniforms and fees. Charlie knew many boys who didn't get to go to school at all.

Soon they reached the center of town. Today was Tuesday—market day. The market place was full of people.

Some were farmers carrying stalks of sweet bananas to sell. Some had baskets of peanuts, called groundnuts by the Ethiopians. Other farmers brought sugar cane, cut up and ready to chew.

One section of the market sold chickens and goats. Another section had colorful lengths of cloth and all sorts of clothing. Near Charlie, a vendor put ears of corn on a grill.

Two women walked past with heavy baskets of grain balanced on their heads. They walked gracefully and easily. They never had to touch the baskets with their hands.

Charlie had tried several times to balance a smaller basket of his mother's on his head, but he had not yet been successful.

A farmer unloaded several unruly goats from a cart. The goats butted each other or dug in and had to be pulled out of the cart. Charlie looked at Wandaro, and they laughed together. The market was as good as a circus, Charlie thought.

Wandaro said, "Let's go see that new stall selling fish."

But the school bell rang, so the boys turned and ran the last of the distance to the school. No one wanted to be late for school. It meant being spanked by the headmaster. And that was not the way to start a Tuesday.

2   Little Treasures

The boys ran through the gate and into the school grounds. There they split up. Charlie and Wandaro sped to the right for the Standard Three class. Biru and Ebbe headed to the left for the Standard One class.

"See you at lunch," called Charlie.

He hurried to get in line with the others in his class. Their teacher gave his signal, and each of the students walked past him, into the classroom. Mr. Mustaffa stood at the door and looked over each uniform. He checked to make sure that each boy was properly and neatly dressed.

A boy whispered behind Charlie. "He always finds something—a shirttail out or a tie crooked."

Getting used to the uniforms, especially the ties, had not been easy for Charlie. He still wasn't sure that he liked living in Ethiopia. He liked his school friends, though. They had a good time playing together.

Sometimes Charlie missed his friends back in Ohio. He missed playing ball with his neighbors Josh and Andy. He missed the Awana Club at his church. He especially missed the snow and the sledding. There was a lot of dust and sand in Ethiopia, but no snow. It was too close to the equator.

The students' uniforms had all been checked. The boys stood by their desks, waiting for Mr. Mustaffa to tell them that they could sit down. That had been different for Charlie too. He remembered his first day at school in Ethiopia when he had come in and sat down immediately. He could still feel the stinging swat that his teacher had given him.

At home, he'd had just one teacher. Here he had three. Mr. Mustaffa taught science during the first hour of the morning. Then another man came to their classroom and taught Amharic for two hours.

Charlie was glad they had recess after Amharic. Right after that, Mr. Salasie came to their classroom to teach history. After lunch, Mr. Mustaffa came back to teach math and then music, their last class of the day.

This morning Charlie decided that he would never understand Amharic. It had two hundred and forty letters in its alphabet.

He spent most of the two-hour period correcting errors on his work sheet. At last the teacher dismissed them for recess.

Outside, he waited for Wandaro, and then the two of them went looking for Biru and Ebbe. They found their friends rolling tires at the end of the playground.

Biru had pulled two tires from the pile that someone had left for the children to play with. One was a truck tire. It was so large that it took two boys to get it rolling and to keep it moving.

Charlie had never rolled tires before he came to Ethiopia. He had learned quickly though, and now it was his favorite playground game.

After a few minutes, he and the other boys left the tires to play soccer. They didn't have a real ball. One of the boys had made a ball by wadding up newspaper and wrapping it with tape. It didn't roll as smoothly as a real soccer ball did, but they could still play a pretty good game.

Charlie's parents had explained to him before they came to Ethiopia that most families didn't have much money. Now that he'd seen the tires and tape balls, he understood better what his parents had meant.

The bell rang, and the boys trudged back to their classrooms. Charlie liked listening to Mr. Salasie. He was a smiling, happy man who found a way to make history very interesting. He seemed to have a story for everything they were learning.

Today Mr. Salasie seemed serious, and his voice was sad. "A group called rebels are trying to take over our country," he said. "They want to get rid of the emperor."

Charlie had seen the emperor once, and he had liked his leopard-skin robe.

Charlie remembered his mother's voice this morning when she had said something about the church. Was she sad because of the rebels too? He didn't know much about politics, but he was sure he didn't like the rebels. They made people too serious and sad.

When I get home, I'm going to ask Dad about the rebels, he thought.

Finally the last class was dismissed, and Charlie met his friends in the school yard. They walked back by the market to see whether any of the vendors were still there.

Many of the vendors were gone, and the rickety tables were empty. The boys wandered past a few stick crates that held chickens. The chickens poked their scrawny white and brown necks through the slats and squawked.

Biru found two feathers beside the cage, and he held them up for the others to see.

"Good treasure," said Charlie, but Biru only smiled at him.

They strolled on into the sections where cloth had been sold. Charlie saw something under one of the tables, and he dropped to his hands and knees.

It was a brown and white bead made of bone. "Treasure," he said. "For my treasure box." He'd put only a feather in his box so far, but someday it would hold many fine things.

He turned the bead over. It was a little smaller than a golf ball. The center was soft, but the outside was carved and shiny. He stuffed the bead into his pocket and caught up with his friends.

3   Quite a Find

Charlie and Wandaro walked on to Wandaro's house. Charlie turned the bone bead over in his hand as they went. It was special. He didn't care that Biru had only glanced at it and said, "No good for a toy."

He played at Wandaro's for about half an hour. Then he ran through the streets to the compound where his family lived. He dragged his book bag in the dust and worked to get the gate open.

The yard was empty. He crossed to the house, calling, "Mom, Dad, I'm home."

Carrie was the only one to meet him as he entered the kitchen. She toddled across the floor and hugged his legs. He pried Carrie loose and hurried into the living room. Maybe someone in there would want to see his treasure from the market place.

Gifati was dusting the tabletop. She stopped when she saw Charlie come in. "Your parents have gone to the hospital with Mrs. Gihuku, but they will be home soon. Your mother left a list of chores for you to do."

Charlie took the list from Gifati. He looked at it as he changed his clothes. Nothing on it was what he wanted to do. He would much rather take his favorite fire engine over to Wandaro's. None of the boys here had ever seen a toy like it—so big and so amazing.

But he turned slowly for the door and his first job—weeding in the garden.

Like all of their neighbors, Charlie's family had a small garden where they grew vegetables and fruits. Charlie liked to eat what came from the garden, but he did not like weeding to help it grow.

He took the hoe from the shed and chopped along the two rows of beans. Small red dust clouds came up with every scratch of the hoe, but the weeds came out too.

Charlie hummed as he worked, and then the hum spilled over into a whistle.

He whistled his favorite songs from Sunday school. Some were songs that he had sung in Ohio. He'd gone to the little church just down the street from Gran and Gramp's house.

He tried not to think of Gran and Gramp because that always made him a little homesick.

He dug harder at the weeds. The clouds of dust rose higher as he poked and jabbed with his hoe. Finally he finished the rows of beans.

Gifati came out the back door and headed toward their cow, Daisy. Charlie dropped his hoe and hurried to join her. He liked to watch Gifati's smooth brown hands coax the milk out of the cow.

Gifati had been teaching him how to milk, and today she let him take a turn at squeezing the white streams of milk into the pail. He had not been at it long when his father called from the gate.

Charlie gave the pail back to Gifati and ran to his father. He showed him the bead he had found.

"My," said his father. He turned the bead over in his fingers. "This was carved by a farmer, or maybe by his wife."

The bead was not quite perfectly smooth, nor perfectly round. It was painted with brown to create a pattern.

"Perhaps it was meant to go into jewelry," Father said. "Quite a find, Son. You'll have to save this in your special box."

"I thought so," said Charlie. "It's as good as the feather I found last week."

"Even better." Father winked, and that made Charlie grin.

"Really? Biru thought it was nothing."

Charlie's father smiled. "Maybe he didn't see how fine this carving is."

Charlie studied his treasure again.

"Why don't you come and help me for a few minutes until supper?" said his father. "I have to mend a broken spot in the compound fence. We might have just about enough time to get it done before we eat."

Charlie set off with his father to get the hammer, some nails, and a board.

He liked the way his father talked to him and the way his father let him do things, not just watch. He was sure there were a lot of things he could do that other boys wouldn't know how to do. Like fixing the fence, or fixing a broken window, or making a chair.

They cut away the old board. Father frowned at the board, but he didn't say anything. Charlie held the new board, and his father hammered it in place. In a pause between hammer blows, Charlie asked his question. "Dad, are those rebels going to come here to our town?"

His father stopped hammering and looked at him. "I don't know, Charlie. What makes you think that?"

Charlie shrugged. "Mr. Salasie was talking about them at school today."

His father began picking up his tools. "We don't know what will happen in the next few days," he said. "But just remember Who's taking care of us." He paused, and Charlie nodded at him.

Then his father said, "How about carrying this hammer for me? Is that your mother calling us for dinner? We'd better get going."

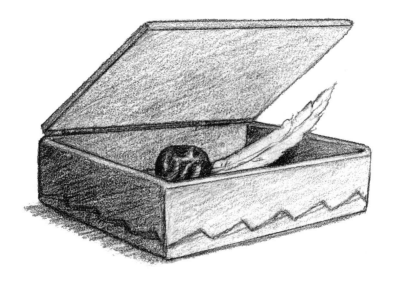

4   Radio Message

Charlie washed his hands carefully. In Ethiopia, a person who was careless about keeping clean could get sick. He wiped a smudge of dirt from his face with a towel and smoothed his hair.

When the family was seated, they held hands with one another around the table and prayed. Charlie's hand always seemed lost in his father's large hand.

His mother's hand was soft and warm. After they finished praying, the hand his mother held always smelled, just a little, like her hand cream.

Charlie looked at the big bowl of food on the table. It was mush, an African dish of peas and cooked cabbage mixed into mashed potatoes. Not his favorite meal, but he was hungry.

He squirmed as his mother put a large spoonful of mush on his plate. He pushed at his food with his fork. Then he asked for a slice of bread and buttered it very slowly. He ate a bite of the bread and then a bit of mush. It was a good plan.

His parents spoke to each other in serious voices, and Charlie tried to listen. He ignored Carrie and her jabbering.

The conversation stopped. Father left his dinner and walked into the living room to answer a call on the shortwave radio.

The crackling and static made it impossible for Charlie to hear the message. This was not the usual time for anyone to call. He ate the last of his mush and waited for his father to return.

When his father came back, he looked serious again. "We're going to be having some company. That was Ned and June Cochrane. There's been some trouble in their town. They're driving down tonight and should be here about ten."

"Gifati," called Charlie's mother. "We're having company in about four hours."

It suddenly became a busy evening. Gifati made the beds in the guest room. Charlie's mother helped him make space in his room for the Cochrane boys. They made two soft pallets on the floor.

"I want to sleep on the floor too," Charlie said. He pulled the pillow and blankets from his bed and spread them on the floor.

His mother nodded at him. "That's fine."

"This will be fun," Charlie said.

His mother straightened up from smoothing the blankets. "The boys will be tired," she said. "You'll have to help them get settled."

"Sure," said Charlie. He wondered how long his friends would stay.

Gifati cooked flat Ethiopian bread and a stew, in case their guests had not eaten.

Charlie couldn't figure out why the Cochranes were coming. Today wasn't a holiday, and they didn't usually visit unless it was a holiday.

Maybe they had trouble with the rebels, he thought.

When it was time for devotions, he came to the kitchen again. He sat by his mother, as usual. She held Carrie, as usual.

Tonight his father read Psalm 91. The words flowed over Charlie like a fine breeze.

He shall give his angels charge over thee,

to keep thee in all thy ways.

Charlie thought about how his father always said this verse when Charlie was afraid.

Because he hath set his love upon me, therefore will I deliver him: I will set him on high, because he hath known my name.

He shall call upon me, and I will answer him: I will be with him in trouble.

Charlie looked at his father. He felt very safe.

5 Company

Charlie's eyes drooped, and his head nodded forward. He sat up straighter in the soft chair. It was almost ten-thirty, and he was still waiting for the Cochranes to arrive.

Charlie's eyes drooped again, and he slid deeper into the chair. A car door slammed, and he was suddenly awake.

His father went to the front door and looked out. He opened the door and walked into the yard to greet their guests.

A few minutes later, his father and Mr. Cochrane came in. They each held the hand of a drowsy boy.

Mrs. Cochrane carried their little girl. She was holding the baby tightly, and she hardly smiled when Charlie's mother said hello.

Charlie was awake enough to greet his friends. "Hi, Tim. Hi, Davy." They weren't as old as he, but they were fun to play with. "I'll show you where we're going to sleep." He led the way to his room.

Tim and Davy were already in their pajamas, and they flopped onto the pallet beds. They were asleep before Charlie's mother turned out the light.

Charlie said his prayers with his father. "Should I pray for Tim and Davy?" Charlie whispered.

His father nodded.

When Charlie had prayed for everyone, his father said, "Sleep well, Charlie boy. I'll see you in the morning."

"What will Tim and Davy do while I'm at school tomorrow?"

"I'm not sure about school tomorrow, Charlie. We'll have to wait and see."

"No school? Is there a holiday?"

"Maybe for you. We'll see. Now—get to sleep." He ruffled Charlie's hair.

"Good night, Dad." Charlie relaxed into the softness of the pillow. A little later he fell asleep, listening to his parents pray.

The next thing Charlie heard was giggling close by. Tim and Davy were laughing and wrestling on their pallets.

Charlie closed his eyes. He wanted to sleep some more. Then he opened his eyes again. The sun was up, and he should be getting ready for school!

He sat up, and the boys pounced upon him.

"Hey, wait! Wait, Davy." Tim and Davy did not wait. They rolled him back onto his pallet and tried to pin him down.

"Get him," said Tim. And both the smaller boys fell onto him, laughing.

Charlie managed to sit up again, and he threw his leg over Davy. Then he got onto one knee, with Davy under him and Tim hanging on his neck.

"Boys!" It was Charlie's mother. "What's going on?"

At once the three stopped and stared at each other.

"See," said Charlie, "we have to stop now." But they all laughed as though someone had told a very good joke.

He dressed quickly and went into the kitchen. His mother and Mrs. Cochrane were sitting at the table drinking coffee. His mother smiled at him. "Good morning, sleepyhead."

"Mom, am I not going to school?"

"It's not as late as you think, Charlie. You can eat breakfast and still meet your friends."

He sat down at the table. Gifati brought him toast and oatmeal. "Is Dad coming in for breakfast?"

"Your father and Mr. Cochrane finished breakfast an hour ago. They're working on the vehicles. They are making sure that the Land Rover is in good condition."

Charlie gulped his food. This was a very unusual day. But things seemed more normal as he joined his friends for the walk to school.

6 An Adventure

At school everything seemed the same. Classes were too long, and recess was too short. But Charlie still wondered why the Cochranes had come. And he thought about what he and Tim and Davy and Wandaro could do when school was out.

History class had just begun when Charlie's father appeared at the classroom door. After a few words with the teacher, he came to Charlie's desk. "Come on, Son; you're leaving school early today."

Charlie's heart beat faster, but all he said was "Okay." He waved good-bye to Wandaro and followed his father out.

"Well," said his father, "are you ready for some adventure?"

Charlie felt better that his father called it an adventure. "I guess so. What are we doing?"

"We're leaving for Kenya. The field director radioed and told us that we were to leave."

"Leave? But why, Dad?"

"You've heard us talking about the rebels in Ethiopia for some time now?"

Charlie nodded.

"A group of men in the army wants to take over the country and get rid of the emperor. Yesterday they came to the town where the Cochranes live. They closed the post office and the school. They began shooting at people who didn't follow their orders."

Charlie felt his stomach tighten, but his father smiled. "We can stay with friends in Nairobi."

Charlie stared at his father. "How long will we be gone?"

"I really don't know," Father said. "We'll have to see what happens before we can decide that."

They crossed the market square.

Then Father said, "When we get home, you'll need to go inside and help your mother pack your clothes. Choose a few of your toys too. We don't have much room, but we want to take as much as we can."

At the compound, Mr. Cochrane had almost finished loading his Land Rover. The luggage rack was full of suitcases and plastic water jugs. There were five gas cans strapped to the rear of the boxes.

Charlie went into the house. He was thinking about what his father had said. He would carry his treasure box with him. But what should he take? It was going to be hard to choose.

He and his mother packed two small suitcases of Charlie's things. She put in plenty of clothes. He chose his favorite books, three trucks, and his large fire engine.

His mother looked long at what he had put in his pile. "There won't be room for the fire engine, Charlie. It's just too big. You'll have to leave it behind."

"But Mom," said Charlie, "it's got to go."

"Charlie, I'm sorry, but it won't fit into a suitcase. There are other things we need to take. There just isn't room for everything."

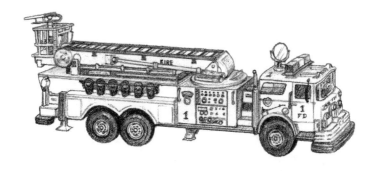

Charlie studied the shiny paint of the engine. His mother stroked his hair. "Besides, we're not leaving forever. We'll be back as soon as things settle down here."

Charlie knew it was useless to argue. He held out the smaller trucks and the books. Mother neatly tucked them into the suitcases among his clothes.

He carried the bags out to the yard, and his
father put them in the back of the Rover.
Charlie and his father carried more suitcases
and boxes out and loaded them into the car.
It quickly grew full.

They stopped for lunch. Gifati had made sandwiches, and Charlie was hungry. He ate two small sandwiches and two bananas. Gifati said nothing as she watched them eat, but tears slid down her cheeks.

Charlie got up and went to stand beside her.

He patted her arm. "Don't cry, Gifati. Mother says that we won't be gone long. We'll be back as soon as things settle down here."

But that only made Gifati cry harder.

7   Going Back

Charlie sat quietly with his treasure box in his lap. He stared out the window as they left the compound. Gifati waved a tearful good-bye, and then she shut the gate.

How long will we be gone? Charlie wondered.

He kept his face pressed to the window so he could see everything that passed. The dirt road was bumpy, and his nose thumped gently against the window with each rock and rut they crossed.

Carrie slept on folded blankets on the floor. She made quiet noises as she squirmed into the softness.

Charlie watched her to see that she was all right, then he gazed out at the passing landscape.

They were climbing into the hills. Charlie's father had told him that the border crossing was in the high country. There would be more rocks and fewer trees with each mile they traveled.

Charlie couldn't help thinking about how hot it was. And he was tired of looking at rocks. His head nodded and slipped forward as he dozed. He woke up when the car stopped.

The car door closed behind his father. He walked back toward the Cochranes' vehicle.

"I want to get out, Mom."

His mother hesitated. "All right," she said at last. "Just stay near your father."

Charlie slid down from the seat and out the door. He walked back to where the two men stood talking.

"I thought about something as I was driving," his father was saying. "Do you think I should've brought the church record books with us? Those rebels are Communists."

Father paused, then he said, "I'm concerned about what might happen to the people. If the rebels are looking for targets, those books would sure make it easy for them."

Mr. Cochrane nodded soberly as he listened. Charlie wondered whether his father meant targets for shooting at.

"I think I should go back," Father said. "We've been traveling for only an hour and a half. I've got plenty of time. If you can squeeze my family into your vehicle, you can cross the border as we planned. I'll join you in just a few hours."

Mr. Cochrane nodded again. "I think you're right, hard as that is to say."

Charlie and his father returned to the car. His mother had a look on her face that he had not seen before. He could not tell whether she was sad or angry. Perhaps she was both.

"What is it?" she asked.

"I'm going back for the records."

Charlie's mother drew in a big breath. His father gave her a kiss on the forehead.

He looked at Charlie. "Come on, Son; I'll need your help in getting things moved to the other vehicle."

Charlie didn't understand all that his father had said. And he didn't like the part he understood. Why was his father going back? How long would he be gone? How would he find them in Kenya?

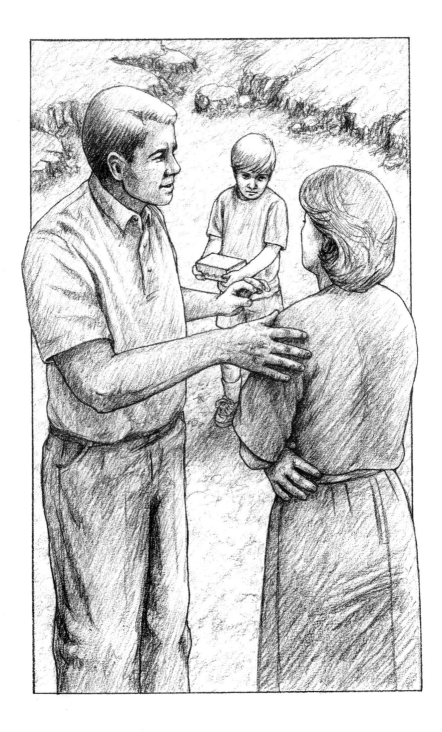

But Charlie didn't ask any of his questions. He just followed his father back to the Land Rover.

The men moved several boxes out of the Cochranes' car, and they put in Charlie's and Carrie's suitcases. Then Charlie's mother and Carrie squeezed into the back seat with Tim and Davy.

Mrs. Cochrane held her baby in the front seat, but there was no room for Charlie. Charlie's mother got out again.

Charlie's parents walked to the front of the Land Rover and talked. Mr. Robinson put his arm around his wife's shoulders. She tucked her head in under his chin, and they talked some more. When they came back, his mother's eyes were wet.

His father said, "Charlie, I guess you're coming with me. It shouldn't take us long to pick up what we need—the church books and more gas—and then we'll meet everyone later tonight in Kenya."

The Cochranes left with Charlie's mother and sister. Charlie stood close to his father and held tightly to his treasure box. His mother waved good-bye, and he waved back.

His father stood silent for a moment, and then he turned and led Charlie back to their Land Rover. They got in, and his father turned the car around, heading back toward the village.

8   Rebels!

The trip back to the village seemed much shorter. Charlie rather liked being on this special mission with his father, whatever the danger. He opened his box and took out the treasure bead.

He held it up to his father. "See, I had room to bring this."

His father glanced over and smiled. Then he gave Charlie's ear a tug and said, "And I had room for my treasure too."

Charlie and his father sang as they traveled. Charlie knew all the words to many hymns.

They sang "He Leadeth Me," his father's favorite.

As they finished singing, they crested the small hill that looked down on the village. They started down the dusty road, and Charlie could see the market place and their compound.

When they arrived at the compound, Charlie jumped out of the car. He opened the gate so his father could drive the Land Rover inside. Gifati had finished her cleaning and had shut and locked the house. She had already gone home.

His father unlocked the back door and went into the kitchen. Charlie followed him. He felt he had been away a long time.

Charlie's father gave him a look, as though he knew how Charlie felt.

"We need to get on our way as quickly as possible," he said. His look softened slightly. "We don't want to keep your mother and Carrie waiting."

"Okay." Charlie ran to his room. There was one thing he wished he could take to Wandaro. His prized fire engine. He was sure Wandaro would take care of it until he came back.

He hurried back to the kitchen, but his father was gone.

Father went to get those books, thought Charlie. And then he made his decision.

It didn't take long to reach Wandaro's house. It was just over one road and a little more toward the edge of town.

Wandaro waved at him through the window and then ran out the door.

"I stopped at your house after school," he said. "But no one was there. Is everything all right?"

"Yes. We're just going to Kenya for a few days. Everyone is worried about the rebels."

Wandaro looked up and down the quiet street. "But why? They aren't here."

"I know, but we have to go. My mom and Carrie went on ahead. I'm here because my father had to come back for something."

"Can you stay for a while and play?"

"A few minutes." Charlie put his treasure box down on one of the stick chairs in the yard. He ran his hands over the red truck. It was still shiny from the last polishing. "This time I didn't bring the truck to play," he said slowly.

I wondered if you would take care of it for me while we're gone. You can use it too."

Wandaro took the truck in his arms. "I will take very good care of it until you return."

"And there is something else," Charlie said. He lightly touched the engine. "If we don't—"

Wandaro's father came up the street. He spoke gruffly to the boys. "Go into the house. Now."

Wandaro jumped up immediately.

Charlie snatched up his treasure box. "Mr. Sassa, I was just—"

"Go," said the man. Charlie stumbled toward Wandaro's house. Wandaro's father caught up with them and took them by the shoulders. He hurried them through the door.

"Papa, what is it?" Wandaro asked.

The man squatted before the boys. "I didn't mean to frighten you or to be unkind. But Charlie, you need to be inside where no one can see you. Does anyone else know you are here?"

"No, sir." Charlie's heart squeezed in upon itself. He felt that something that he could not see was about to fall on him.

"Good," said Wandaro's father. "You will have to trust me and do what I say. Two trucks of rebel soldiers drove into the village a few minutes ago. The first place they went was the church."

Charlie could not hold his questions any longer. "Where is my father?"

Wandaro's father took Charlie by his shoulders. "They have arrested your father."

The room seemed to swirl around Charlie, and the words repeated themselves: *arrested your father, arrested your father.*

Wandaro's father was still talking. "I will go back and see what can be found out. But I wanted to make sure you were safe first. I saw you in the Rover with your father and thought you might be here."

Charlie wasn't crying, but he knew it would be easy for him to do so. He turned away and rubbed his eyes. His breath came out hard in a big whoosh, and he felt dizzy.

"Charlie." Wandaro's father was waiting.

Charlie slowly turned and looked at his friend's father. He nodded.

He was afraid he would cry if he tried to say anything.

"Stay inside. Both of you." Wandaro's father looked sternly at Wandaro.

Wandaro and Charlie both answered, "Yes sir."

Wandaro's father stood and strode out, shutting the door behind him.

Charlie sat down, straight down upon the floor. He said nothing.

Wandaro stood looking first at the closed door and then at Charlie.

"Charlie" he said, and then he stopped.

Charlie closed his eyes to pray.

9   A Spy?

Charlie didn't know how long he had been sitting on the floor praying. It felt like a long time since Wandaro's father had left. He thought that when he opened his eyes, it might already be dark outside.

It wasn't. Wandaro stood watching him. "Are you all right?" asked his friend.

"I think so."

"Are you afraid?"

Charlie nodded. "But I'm sure my father will be here soon. He's only a missionary. Why would the soldiers want to keep him? It's just a mistake."

"Yes—it must be a mistake." A moment passed, and Wandaro brightened a little. "Do you want to play with your truck?"

"No, I don't think so." Charlie moved to a chair and sat quietly. He wished his mother were here. She would know what to do. Even with Wandaro there, Charlie felt very alone.

Wandaro left the room. Soon he came back, holding a small green book. It was a New Testament that Charlie had given him.

"Here. Your father says the Bible can always help us. You can use mine."

Charlie took the book and held it tightly. He remembered a verse he had memorized with his parents. *He shall call upon me, and I will answer him.* Charlie wanted his father to be there, to call upon the Lord for him.

It seemed that Wandaro's father would never return. The patch of sky Charlie could see through the window turned gray. Then it became a dark blue-black. Wandaro's mother made supper, and the boys ate.

Charlie could not taste the food, and he did not feel hungry. Still Wandaro's father did not come back.

Wandaro did his homework, and Charlie watched his friend. He watched the door too. He was looking at the door when Wandaro's father entered.

The man's eyes were dark, and his mouth was in a straight line. He crossed the room to where Charlie sat and squatted before the boy. Charlie did not take his eyes from the man's face.

"I'm afraid my news is not good," Wandaro's father said.

He waited, and when Charlie said nothing, he went on. "When I got back to the church, the soldiers and your father were gone. I went to the market to see what I could hear."

Wandaro's father looked back toward the door where his wife stood. Then he turned to Charlie. "Just a few minutes later the soldiers passed through. They had your father and the shortwave radio from your house." He took a breath and let it out. "They think he is a spy. The radio is their proof."

Charlie heard the words, but he could not make sense of them. A spy? Everyone knew that his father was just a missionary.

Charlie felt tears trickle down his cheeks. He could not stop himself.

Wandaro's father put his hand on Charlie's arm. "There will be a trial in the morning. We must wait until then to see what must be done."

Charlie could only nod. A sob escaped him. Wandaro's mother came and patted his shoulder. Wandaro's father stood and went into the kitchen.

Charlie thought about his father and then about his mother and Carrie. He knew his mother would start to worry soon. What would she think when they didn't get there tonight?

"My mother will be worried," he said.

Wandaro's mother said, "There is nothing to do until tomorrow. And already it is time for bed. You and Wandaro can sleep in here."

She had prepared blankets for him on the floor in Wandaro's bedroom.

Charlie knew he would not be able to sleep, but he lay down anyway. He put his treasure box on the floor next to him. He tried for a moment to think, and he found that he was very tired. He wished terribly that his father would come in and say, "Sleep well, Charlie boy." He tried to say a long prayer, and somewhere in the night he fell asleep.

10 Guilty

Charlie awoke in the strange room. Wandaro was already sitting up next to him. Then Charlie remembered. His first thoughts were of his father.

Wandaro's father was already gone when the boys went into the kitchen. Charlie ate the bread and bananas slowly. He was still thinking about his father.

And what about his mother. What was she thinking? How would he get to her if . . . ? No, nothing was going to happen to his father.

A whoop from Wandaro brought Charlie back to the moment.

"What?" said Charlie.

Wandaro pulled his excitement in. "I'm sorry," he said. "Mother says I don't have to go to school."

"Oh," Charlie said.

They folded up Charlie's blanket bed so there would be a place to play. Wandaro's mother reminded them they were not to go outside. Then she left to go to the market.

Charlie sat with his back against the wall and his knees drawn up to his chest. Wandaro moved the fire truck around the floor, but he did not ring its bell or use the water hoses. It reminded Charlie that none of the boys had known what a fire truck was.

He had tried to explain, but he still wasn't sure they understood.

Time dragged by. Several sounds made Charlie look up, thinking Wandaro's father must be back. Finally Wandaro's mother returned from the market. After a few words to the boys, she went to work in the garden. The rhythmic sounds of her hoe filtered into the house.

Charlie grew tired of sitting inside. He wanted to go and see what was happening with his father. He wanted to do something.

Lunch time passed, and still no word came from Wandaro's father. Charlie felt more and more like a balloon that was too full and about to burst. He walked through the house and then sat again on the floor. He took the bead out of his treasure box and flicked it with his finger. It rolled back and forth.

It was then that Wandaro's father returned. He first went to the kitchen. He picked up some flat bread and chewed it, then he got a drink of water. At last, he turned back to Charlie.

Charlie's stomach knotted into a ball as Wandaro's father approached him.

"They had the trial, Charlie." The man put his hand to his brow, rubbing it slowly. "Your father and five other men were found guilty of being spies."

He looked away from Charlie. After a long time he spoke again, just barely above a whisper. "They plan to execute them tomorrow morning."

11 Tested Treasure

"That can't happen!" shouted Charlie. It was the bluntness of Wandaro's father that seemed to pull the words from his mouth.

Wandaro's mother went to him. "Hush, Charlie. We still do not want people to know you are here."

Wandaro's father said, "You are right, Charlie. It cannot be permitted for these criminals to execute your father."

"But what can we do?" Charlie felt his whole body must be on fire.

"Charlie, we have plans," said Wandaro's father. "We want to rescue your father tonight.

Then we will get both of you to the border. I will need some help from you. We need to get a message to your father."

Wandaro's father looked about the room. "We need something that will let him know that you are well and that he can trust us. Your father will not know all of the men whom he may see."

Charlie thought for a moment. He looked down at his shoes, and his gaze fell upon the treasure box. He remembered the bead. His father had seen it. His father knew that it was his treasure.

Charlie held out the bead. "We could use this," he said softly.

Wandaro's father took the bead. It disappeared easily in his large hand. "Your father knows this?" he said.

Charlie nodded. "Yes."

Wandaro's father took the bead to the kitchen and found a sharp knife. He cut away the cork that had been used as filler in the center hole. It left a large smooth hole about as big around as a pencil.

"We can put a note in this space and get the bead to your father." He took a small piece of paper and handed it to Charlie. "You write. He will know your hand."

Charlie wrote what Wandaro's father said. *"Trust the man who carries the bead."*

Wandaro's father prepared to leave again. He turned to Charlie. "You also may not recognize the man who will come for you later. Trust the man who carries the bead."

12 God's Man

The afternoon faded into evening. Charlie ate the supper prepared for him. He waited for something to happen, but he didn't know what. He heard strange sounds in the night, but no one went out to investigate.

The boys played *Mancala* quietly on the floor. Charlie moved his stones without much thought, and he quickly lost two games to Wandaro. They started a third game.

Wandaro's mother came in to check on them. "It will soon be over, Charlie. You must wait a little longer."

Charlie turned back to the board and made his next play. It took just a few minutes more to lose a third game.

He decided not to play again.

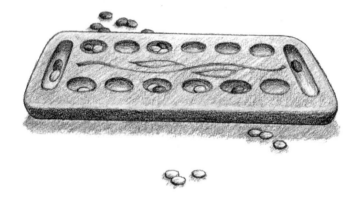

Wandaro started a wrestling tussle. His mother let them wrestle. Their play lasted only a few minutes, but afterwards both boys were more settled.

It was time for bed. Again the blankets were spread on the floor.

"Charlie, leave all of your clothes on tonight," Wandaro's mother said. "We do not know what will happen or when. You must be ready to go at any moment I call for you."

"Yes ma'am."

She turned out the light and left the room. Charlie lay on the blankets, trying to guess what would happen. How would the men rescue his father? He turned toward the window and thought of his mother.

He said softly and with effort, "*He shall call upon me, and I will answer him.*" Charlie closed his eyes tight.

I must call for myself, he thought.

He prayed with all his might for his mother and sister. He prayed for his father and the men who planned to rescue him.

He must have dozed. The blankets became twisted under him as he flopped about.

Charlie sat up, startled awake by a touch on his shoulder. His heart pounded, for it was not Wandaro's mother. Over him stood a tall soldier dressed in green. His eyes were nearly covered by the hat pulled low on his forehead.

Charlie didn't know whether he should scream or try to run. He stared up at the man.

"Come with me," the man said softly.

Charlie felt that his arms and legs were stone. They did not obey him. Was he being arrested too? What would happen to him?

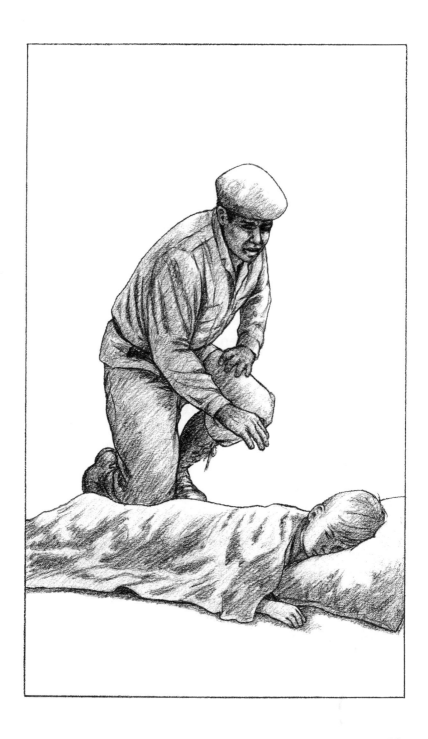

The man opened his hand, and the bead lay cupped in his palm.

Two more men in uniform waited outside. The four of them walked quickly to the compound where Charlie's family lived. They entered and shut the gate behind them.

Charlie was surprised to see that the back door was standing open. There were clothes and furniture lying about the yard. The Rover was still there, but most of the suitcases and boxes had been taken from it.

Charlie started toward the house, but one man stopped him. "Better to wait out here."

So he sat down on the back bumper of the Rover and held his treasure box close to his chest. There were only blankets in the back of the car.

A truck stopped outside, and one of the uniformed men opened the gate for it. Some men got out of the truck. There were two soldiers he did not know, and then Wandaro's father.

The last man got out. His father!

Charlie ran toward him. His father opened his arms, then he closed them tightly around Charlie. He lifted Charlie in a hug. His father did not put him down—he carried him across the yard to the Land Rover.

"Dad, I was—"

"I know, Son." His father put him in the rear cargo space and climbed in after him. One of the soldiers spread the blankets over them and shut the rear gate.

Charlie snuggled against the warmth of his father, who held him tightly. "They will drive us out of town with the truck following," said his father.

"But how did they get the truck and the uniforms?"

"I don't know. And our Land Rover was still here. Our passports were still lying on the front seat. That is a miracle, Charlie."

The Rover bucked over the rough roads. Charlie was content to lie in his father's arms. He didn't stir until his father shook him awake. The rear gate was open, and his father was standing next to Wandaro's father.

"Here," the man was saying. "Your records."

Charlie's father took the packet, and then he clasped the man's hand. "Thank you."

Charlie shivered in the cold air.

"Look, Son." His father pointed down the road. "That's the border station. We're almost to Kenya!"

"We thought it would be safest if we brought you this far." Wandaro's father smiled down at Charlie.

Charlie looked up at him. "Thank you, sir."

"You are most welcome, my child. Your father is God's man, and he is still needed to preach. I am glad that God could use me to help your father."

"Could you say good-bye to Wandaro for me?" asked Charlie. "I didn't get to tell him myself."

"That I will." The man knelt before Charlie. "I have something for you." He opened his hand, and the brown and white bead rolled out into Charlie's hand. "Keep this to remember us by. Come back to us. There are many people here who still need to know the Lord—and you could tell them."

Charlie's fingers closed over the bead. "Good-bye," he said. Wandaro's father walked him to the front of the Land Rover and helped him onto the seat.

His father started the engine, and the car slowly rolled forward. Charlie turned to watch behind them.

The men waved once, then they got into their truck and started back up the road.

Charlie rubbed the bead with his thumb. I will come back, he thought. I will come back and preach God's Word.

He glanced at his father and then returned his gaze to the road ahead. "Hey, Dad, look! There's Mr. Cochrane's Rover on the other side."

"So it is," said his father. He pulled to a stop at the border crossing. "And there are two girls waiting for us on the other side too." He tugged Charlie's ear. "Let's go see them, Charlie boy."